Grand

Bread

VISTA®
HIGHER LEARNING

Boston, Massachusetts

Nadia is 15 years old. Her favorite activity is cooking. Adam is Nadia's friend. He likes cooking, too. They're taking a cooking class. They really enjoy it!

Mr. Harvey is their teacher. He says, "There is a bread baking contest. It's on Saturday. Please come!"

Nadia

Adam

Mr. Harvey

FLOUR

"Do you want to be in the contest?" asks Adam.

"Yes!" answers Nadia. "What can we make?"

"I want to make bread," says Adam. "But I don't know how."

"I know!" says Nadia. "Let's make Grandma Bread!"

BREAD-BAKING CONTEST

ALL BAKERS ARE WELCOME!

YEAST BREAD

QUICK BREADS

BUN AND ROLLS

INTERNATIONAL BREADS

SATURDAY JANUARY 29TH
AT 12:30
MR. HARVEY'S COOKING S

It's a bread baking contest. People make bread. The best bread wins.

"What's 'Grandma Bread'?" asks Adam.

"My Grandma Olga lives in Russia," says Nadia. "She makes great bread. My favorite bread is Grandma Bread!"

"OK," says Adam. "Do you have the recipe?"

"Um . . . no," says Nadia. "Let's call Grandma. She can help."

This is Nadia's grandma. She is the mother of Nadia's father.

"Hi, Grandma!" says Nadia.

"Nadia! How are you?" says Grandma Olga.

"I'm fine," answers Nadia. "There is a baking contest. We want to make Grandma Bread. Can you send the recipe, please?"

"Sure," says Grandma Olga. "I'll send it now. Good luck!"

"Thanks!" says Nadia.

Adam and Nadia go to the kitchen. They wait.
Bing! Nadia looks at her phone. It's the recipe!
"Come on, Adam," says Nadia. "Time to make
Grandma Bread!"

Grandma Bread

1 Egg

300 g Flour

30 g Baking Soda

7 g Salt

15 g Sugar

60 g Butter

240 g Cheese

240 ml Milk

scale

They look at the recipe. "One egg, flour . . . wait," says Adam. "What's 300 **g**? And *M-L*?"

"Uh-oh," says Nadia. "It's metric."

"Oh no!" says Adam. "Our **scale** is from the U.S."

"No problem," says Nadia. "We can find US equivalents."

7

"Right," says Adam. "First, 300 grams of flour."

"OK," says Nadia. "So, 1,000 grams is one kilogram. One kilogram is 2.2 pounds." Nadia uses her **calculator**. "So, 100 grams is 3.53 ounces."

"OK. So, 300 grams is about 11 ounces," says Adam.

calculator

bowl

MILK

SUGA

Adam **weighs** the flour. He puts it in a bowl.

"Next we add 30 grams of baking soda," says Nadia. She uses her calculator. "That's 1.1 ounces. Let's round down to one ounce."

"Got it!" says Adam. "You're right, Nadia. This is easy!"

weighing
flour

Baking soda makes bread higher.

Nadia finds the equivalents. Adam makes the bread. Soon the bread is almost ready. "It looks great!" says Nadia. She puts the bread in a pan.

"What **temperature**?" Adam asks.

Nadia looks at the recipe. "It says 200 **degrees** for 40 minutes."
"Got it!" Adam says.

temperature

200 ° F

degrees

pan

oven

The oven gets hot. Nadia puts in the bread.

Adam and Nadia clean up. Then, they wait. Soon they hear *Ring!* It's the timer. The Grandma Bread is ready!

timer

Nadia takes out the bread. It looks strange!
Adam cuts the bread. It's very soft! Nadia
tastes the bread. It tastes like flour!
"Oh no!" says Adam. "What's wrong?
More flour? More eggs?"

"I don't know," says Nadia.
"I'll call Grandma."

"Hi Grandma," says Nadia. "We made your bread. But something's wrong."

"What?" asks Grandma Olga.

"Well, the recipe was metric. But we found US equivalents. I know *they're* right," says Nadia. "The bread is soft. It tastes strange!"

"Soft? Strange?" says Grandma. "Did you bake it?"

"Yes," says Nadia. "We baked it 40 minutes at 200 degrees."

"Wait," says Grandma. "At 200 degrees *Celsius*?"

"Oh no!" says Nadia. She looks at Adam. "We changed the recipe. We didn't change the temperature. It was 200 degrees **Fahrenheit**!"

200° Fahrenheit = 93° Celsius
200° Celsius = 392° Fahrenheit

"Well there's your answer," says Grandma, laughing.

"Now I understand!" says Nadia. "Thanks, Grandma!"

"No problem," says Grandma Olga. "What about the contest?"

"Time to make more bread," says Nadia. "And use the right temperature!"

g = gram = .035 ounces

scale

calculator

weigh (flour)

temperature

degree

0° Celsius
=
32° Fahrenheit

Celsius

0° Fahrenheit
=
-18° Celsius

Fahrenheit